Off We Go!

First published in 2010
by Wayland

Text copyright © Louise John
Illustration copyright © Catalina Alvarez

Wayland
338 Euston Road
London NW1 3BH

Wayland Australia
Level 17/207 Kent Street
Sydney, NSW 2000

Series Editor: Louise John
Editor: Katie Powell
Cover design: Paul Cherrill
Design: D.R.ink
Consultant: Shirley Bickler

A CIP catalogue record for this book is available from the British Library.

ISBN 9780750261869

Printed in China

Wayland is a division of Hachette Children's Books,
an Hachette UK Company

www.hachette.co.uk

Off We Go!

Written by Louise John
Illustrated by Catalina Alvarez

WAYLAND

"Off we go on holiday!"
said Mum.

5

"I am going to play in the sand on holiday," said Olly.

"Have you got your bucket?" said Dad.

"Oh, no!" said Olly.

"Back we go," said Dad.

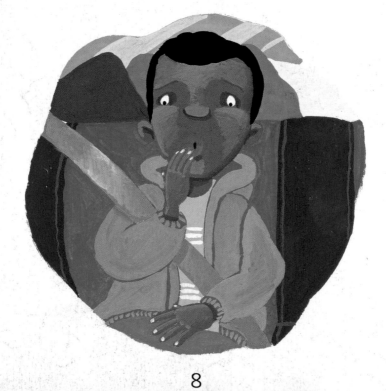

9

"I am going to swim in the pool on holiday," said Cara.

"Have you got your swim ring?" said Dad.

"Oh, no!" said Cara.

"Back we go, again," said Dad.

"I am going to sit in the sun on holiday," said Mum.

"Have you got your sunglasses?" said Dad.

"No, I haven't," said Mum.

"Back home we go," said Dad.

"Off we go on holiday, again," said Mum.

"Oh, no!" said Dad.
"Too late!"

Guiding a First Read of
Off We Go!

It is important to talk through the book with the child before they read it alone. This prepares them for the way the story unfolds, and allows them to enjoy the pictures as you both talk naturally, using the language they will later encounter when reading. Read them the brief overview, and then follow the suggestions below:

1. Talking through the book
The family were setting off to the airport on holiday. Oh no, Olly had forgotten his bucket, so they went back for that. Cara had forgotten her swim ring, and Mum realised she didn't have her sunglasses. Do you think they caught the plane? Let's see.

Let's read the title: **Off We Go!**
On page 4, the family were ready to set off to the airport. And on page 6, Olly was thinking about playing in the sand on holiday.
"Have you got your bucket?" said Dad.
Did he have it? "Oh, no!" said Olly.
"Back we go," said Dad.

Continue through the book, guiding the discussion to fit the text as the child looks at the illustrations.

On page 18, they set off on holiday yet again.
Turn the page. Can you see their plane taking off?
"Oh, no! Too late!"

22

2. A first reading of the book

Ask the child to read the book independently, pointing carefully underneath each word (tracking), while thinking about the story. Praise attempts by the child to correct themselves, and prompt them to use their letter knowledge, the punctuation, and check the meaning, for example:

You said, "The family were sitting off." Does that make sense? It looks like 'sitting', but read it carefully again and think what would make sense.

That's a question mark. Try to make it sound like Dad asking a question. Well done.

3. Follow-up activities

The high frequency words in this title are:

am	go	going	got	have	I	in	no
off	on	play	said	the	to	we	you

- Select two high frequency words, and ask the child to find them throughout the book. Discuss the shape of the letters and their letter sounds.
- To memorise the words, ask the child to write them in the air, then write them repeatedly on a whiteboard or on paper, leaving a space between each attempt.

4. Encourage

- Reading the book again — with expression.
- Drawing a picture based on the story.
- Writing one or two sentences using the practised words.

23

START READING is a series of highly enjoyable books for beginner readers. **The books have been carefully graded to match the Book Bands widely used in schools.** This enables readers to be sure they choose books that match their own reading ability.

Look out for the Band colour on the book in our Start Reading logo.

The Bands are:

Pink Band 1A & 1B

Red Band 2

Yellow Band 3

Blue Band 4

Green Band 5

Orange Band 6

Turquoise Band 7

Purple Band 8

Gold Band 9

START READING books can be read independently or shared with an adult. They promote the enjoyment of reading through satisfying stories supported by fun illustrations.

Louise John is really the editor of Start Reading, but wanted to see how she liked writing books, too. It was quite tricky, but she found that eating lots of chocolate biscuits made her think better! She tries out her ideas on her daughter, Amelia, who tells her if they are any good or not!

Catalina Alvarez lives in Sherwood, Nottingham with her son Oscar and two cats called Lizzie and Winnie. She has illustrated more books than she can count, especially lots of phonics books. Her favourite one is called 'Pog the Dog!'